Keith Martin

THE ABSOLUTE BOTTOM LINE

Staple
NEW WRITING
1999

THE ABSOLUTE
BOTTOM LINE

Keith Martin

ISBN 1 901185 01 X

TYPESET
by
ROGER BOOTH ASSOCIATES
HASSOCKS, WEST SUSSEX
IN NEW BASKERVILLE

PRINTED
at
THE ARC & THROSTLE PRESS
NANHOLME MILL, TODMORDEN

DESIGN
by
BILL AND LUCY BERRETT

PUBLISHED
by
Staple NEW WRITING
25 MARCH 1999

Staple
is published with
financial assistance
from East Midlands
Arts

For Ruth and Lynsey

Do not let any sweet-talking woman beguile your good sense

with the fascination of her shape. It's your barn she's after.

Hesiod, Works and Days

CONTENTS

Night Shift	7
Andy's Effort	15
The Absolute Bottom Line	17
Jim, My Ex-Neighbour	25
Schizo John and Al	33
Summer Lightning	35
Was That Your Wife and Daughter?	45
Five Fags and Four Cans of Lager	53
The Flood	57
Keith Martin	58
Staple New Writing	59

NIGHT SHIFT

Somebody tapped me on the shoulder. I looked round, nodded and, because I hadn't shut off the gun, accidentally put pressure on the trigger and it clacked off on its own. I jumped aside. He raised his eyes, shook his head and looked away down the tunnel. I reached and found the switch by the connecting hose that turned the gun off, pulled up the hoses and laid the gun on the floor. I twisted out the earplugs.

It was suddenly loud. There was a sharp hissing from the hoses. The gun slipped slightly, where the floor was curved.

'They said they can't get to sleep up there,' he said.

I pinched my nose. There was dust everywhere. I wondered who he was.

'What?'

'They're trying to get to sleep.'

I took off my helmet and wiped sweat off my brow with my arm. The dust stuck to me. He wasn't wearing a helmet. He was wearing a scruffy baggy blue jumper and gloves. His hair was fairly long and straggly. I pinched my nose again, to stop myself sneezing.

I shrugged. 'Well... I don't know what to do.'

'Didn't they give you a mask?'

'No?'

'They normally do.' He turned and walked away.

I didn't know what to do. There was dust everywhere – cement dust floating in the air. Somebody had said... 'They're supposed to bring round lime juice.' In the hut while we'd been getting ready. This bald man who had been sitting at a table at the far end, his face covered with black grime – apart from the stripe round his eyes, where he had been wearing goggles – and the clean dome of his bald head from the safety helmet. He was halfway through a double shift, sitting at the table, drinking tea from a flask. 'By law,' he added, in an authoritative tone. And I had looked over, partly out of politeness, seeing as nobody else seemed to be taking any notice of him.

Another bloke, getting ready, climbing into his overalls, said: 'Oh yeah, they'll bring you the full breakfast too!'

'By law!' the bald man at the table said.

The other man tutted.

'There's asbestos in there as well,' another man who was getting ready chimed in.

'We're all going to die one way or another,' the second man said.

I waited for a while. Wondering. There was no one about to ask. Those who knew the score. Earlier there had been loads of people around, in this area – small huddles of men, looking around and discussing things. It was dark, despite strings of light bulbs along each side – only half of them working. White dust flew around each bulb and some light came up from a hatch at the bottom. Every sound echoed. In the distance along the round tunnel there were the shadows of people moving about in the section of the kiln where the chains hung. Apart from the noise coming from there – like a constant background hum, and the tapping of trowels beyond that – it was silent and it was chilly and dark. It was one of those moments in life when you ask yourself: What the fuck am I doing here?

I coughed and the sound bounced round the steel walls. The man in the blue jumper had walked off in the other direction, away from the end of the kiln with the light and the chains. Beyond that they were bricking in the kiln, working from that way down. You couldn't smoke in here, only outside. I had my fags in my shirt pocket beneath the overall. I felt the bulge of the square pack and sat down. I wondered what the time was. This was night one. Assuming I stayed the course – and, man, I needed the money – I had eleven more nights of this, eleven more nights of twelve-hour shifts. A long stretch like that can look like nothing looking back. Not everybody stayed the course, one of the blokes in the hut had said, in a general way – but, I reckoned, just for my benefit. Fridays and Saturdays were particularly under-attended, he'd said.

I sat down by the gun. It was a jackhammer running off two hoses that came up through the hatch at the bottom of the kiln. The compressor was running below but you could only hear that over by the hatch. You couldn't get out that way though. The only way out and in was through another hatch further along that had a ladder going down to the ground. The bloke who had led me up here, who I took to be the foreman, had pointed to the panels on the side where the cement had hardened and stuck. The gun was already there. 'Just clean all that off,' he said. Then he held up his arm and stared at his watch. (I had taken that to mean that he was timing me.) 'And keep your helmet on at all times,' he added. 'In case he comes along. He sometimes sneaks around at night to catch people out.'

I wondered if that had been him, previously. Blue Jumper. At least I'd had my helmet on. The man who had led me up here was Jim. He seemed all right. 'They employ a certain amount of casual labour,' he'd told me, as we'd been walking over, under the kilns. 'To cover themselves. One bloke's on holiday this week.' He stopped at the foot of the ladder, scratched his nose and dropped his voice to a whisper. 'What I'm saying is,' he said, looking around, 'if you are scratching on, you wanna be careful about whose name you give.' He'd looked at me. 'I just need the money,' I said, shrugging. 'Pay off some debts.' 'Well,' he said. 'You know. It goes on. And you can't trust no bastard round here.' Then he'd turned and climbed the ladder.

I waited for a while. It was deserted this end. Along to my right shadows moved through the chains. I wished I'd worn a watch. I didn't have a watch but I wished that I'd thought to buy a cheap one – thought about that before. I would have known then when the first tea break was. I hadn't really expected to be put somewhere completely on my own on the first night. I waited for a long time and then I stood up, brought out some earplugs, unwrapped and inserted them. It felt funny at first; as if you were locked inside your own head. I picked up the gun, looked left and right and turned the switch and pulled the trigger back on the handle. The chisel at the end slid up the hardened cement and then found a groove by a lip of the steel. I pushed on the gun and started hammering. The dust flew.

I was sweating. The dust was flying. Then, after about ten minutes it happened again – the tap on the shoulder. I looked round. It was him: Blue Jumper. He looked serious, annoyed. I turned the switch and stopped the gun, laid it down and twisted out my earplugs. He stood facing me, his hands on his hips.

'What are you doing?'

I swallowed. 'Jim told me I have to clean all this off,' I said, pointing to where I'd been gunning.

'They're trying to get their heads down.'

'Who are?'

'The lads.'

'What lads?'

'The welders and that up top.'

'Well,' I said. 'Jim told me…'

'And who the fuck's this Jim?'

'The foreman, I suppose.'

'Well… tell Jim I told you.'

'Well… who are you then…?'

'Bert. Tell Jim that Bert told you to give the gun a rest, knock it off. Right?'

I shrugged.

'Right?'

'I suppose so,' I said. I shrugged. Bert glared at me.

'You wanna ask them for a mask – don't let them fob you off. They're always trying to cut corners, to save pennies. And there are rules and regulations.'

'Right,' I said. 'I've only just started here, don't really know what's what.'

'What are you, local?' He put up one foot on the metal lip of the inner wall and leaned, resting his arm on his knee.

'Dartford.'

'Dartford! I used to go to the dogs, at Crayford.'

'That's near,' I said, wiping off sweat.

'Keith Richards came from Dartford you know.' He held out one arm. 'Jajang!' He made a guitar noise and played an invisible chord. 'In my opinion he's the governor, straight chords. None of that fanny dancing shit. Disco!' He spat. 'And none of your fiddly-diddly Clapton. Neil Young as well, he's alright.' He turned and walked away.

I sat down again, by the gun. I waited. I wished that I had thought to ask Bert the time. I sat there for what seemed like ages. I pushed back the helmet on my head and pinched my nose to stop myself sneezing. Along the tunnel shadows moved through the lit-up part among the chains. From beyond that came the regular tap tap tap, where they were bricking round the kiln. I wished that I knew where Jim was so that I could get it sorted out. The trouble was I didn't know anything. I didn't even know the proper way in and out of the site. I had come through a hole in the fence by the bus stop and then slid down a steep bank to reach a row of portakabins. Asked for Mr Ashby, like I had been told to, and been directed to the last portakabin in the row; a scruffy grey one, not freshly painted blue like all the others. In the grey porta-kabin I had found a ginger-haired man who looked as if he had just woken up. 'Yes?' he said stroppily. He took down details. 'Start tonight then,' he said. 'Tonight?' 'Yes, tonight. OK?' And this evening, Jim, who had come into the hut at a quarter to six, had sent all the other blokes off here and there and led me down across an open yard and some rail tracks and under the massive kilns: five horizontal metal cylinders suspended in the air, about two hundred yards long. Three of them revolving and throwing off heat and the two at the end still – 'down' as they say. Then up the ladder, through a hatch and we were inside the end kiln.

I had to find Jim. That was the best thing. I stood up and walked along to the hatch in the bottom of the kiln. The hatch was surrounded by a scaffold safety-rail. I got down on my knees. Then I took off my helmet and lay flat on the metal floor, crawled forward under the lower rail and stuck my head through and looked out from the bottom of the kiln. It was night and, apart from the compressor humming and some background banging and crashing, there was an air of stillness. Of course, looking out everything was upside down. I could see the occasional sudden blue flash of welders' torches, and the lights on the chimneys pointing down to the dark cloud-filled sky and reflecting out on the black river above.

I stood up again, brushing myself off. Then I picked up the helmet and walked along to the far end, where we'd come in.

Outside, at the bottom of the ladder, I took off the helmet, leaned against some large metal pipes that were stacked there and lit up a fag. It was chillier than I had expected it to be. I leaned in the half-light and smoked a whole cigarette. I didn't see a soul. In a few hours, I thought, it'll start getting light.

A bucket emerged. A plastic yellow bucket came out from another hatch, at the bottom of the kiln about sixty feet along from where I was leaning, smoking my second fag. The bucket floated silently through the air. It was on a rope, tied on the handle. I watched it float down and settle on the ground. The bucket sat there for a while. Then a white face poked out from the hatch.

'Are you there?'

I looked around.

'Put us some half-laps in there, Bert,' the face shouted at me.

'I'm not Bert,' I said, half-grinning. I walked down underneath the kiln towards him.

'Eh?'

I cupped my mouth and shouted. 'I'm not Bert!'

'No need to shout. I'm not deaf. Half-laps!' he shouted. His hand came out and pointed. 'There, by the bucket.'

I shrugged and went to where he pointed. Next to where the bucket had settled lay a pile of scaffolding fittings, various types. I took one off the top of the pile and held it up to show him.

'This?' I said. The head shook impatiently.

'Half-laps! Or DHs'll do!'

I bent to pick up another type of fitting. Then there was a loud, sudden roaring noise, from out of the darkness. A forklift, lights blazing, came across the yard towards me, shot past and disappeared again, into the darkness. 'Watch out, Bains is about!' a voice shouted. When I looked up the face at the hatch had gone.

A man came strolling along, out of the darkness. A young, skinny bloke in jeans and a t-shirt. He was smoking a roll-up. 'Oh yeah?' he said. 'Oh yeah? Oh yeah? Think you're it?' He hunched his shoulders in a hard way and walked right up to me. Then, noticing the yellow bucket and the rope, he looked up. 'What d'you want, Bert?' he shouted.

'Ah ha! Is that you, Bert?' a voice shouted down.

'He thought I was Bert,' I said.

The bloke said, 'Er?' He glanced at me and then up. The white face appeared.

'Half-laps!'

The bloke put his fag in his mouth and hurriedly filled the bucket with a certain type of fitting. Then, removing the fag, he whistled and tugged on the rope. 'Yow!' he shouted.

The white face had gone. The man grinned at me. A shout of 'yow' came back as the rope went taut. The bloke at the bottom pushed up the bucket and it rose up in the sky and disappeared in the hatch. He turned and grinned again.

'Easy as that,' he said. He exhaled and raised his eyes. 'Pleasant evening,' he said.

I nodded, warily. 'D'you know someone called Jim?'

'Jim who?'

'I don't know. Jim with a moustache.'

'Rings a bell,' he said, quickly. He smiled broadly and then, immediately, frowned. 'Nope! I've never seen him before in my life! I was there but it wasn't me, Officer! Wink, wink.' He looked at me. 'What are you, a policeman?'

'No.' I started to explain. 'This bloke Jim...'

He interrupted me. 'You on the lookout for a bit of gear then? Is that it?'

There was a shout from above, 'Beelow!' The yellow bucket floated down again.

I was standing by the ladder, leaning on the pipes smoking, when Jim appeared. I heard footsteps and looked around and he was coming up behind me under the kiln.

'What d'you think of it so far then?' he said, chirpily. 'Where you been? You missed tea. Nobody tell you?'

I turned to him. 'No,' I said. 'Actually...'

'I've got another job, if you've finished that. Cushier.'

'I haven't finished it,' I said.

Jim gave me a look. He went to look at his watch but stopped himself.

'Someone called Bert told me to knock it off,' I said quickly.

Jim looked at me. He lifted his helmet and wiped his brow. He stroked his chin. 'Well... you don't just go taking notice of anybody who comes along,' he said.

'Well... he came along twice!' I said, sort of annoyed.

Jim scratched his head and thought some more. He scratched his ear, sighed, folded his arms. There was a noise, a rising echo of footsteps. We both looked round. A man came walking up towards us from under the kilns. It was the ginger-haired man from earlier, wearing a helmet, trousers and a clean nylon shirt.

'Jim,' he said. He stopped. He had a pen in his shirt pocket. He glanced at me as if to say, I've seen you before somewhere, haven't I? and then looked at Jim. 'How's it going?'

'All right, Frank,' Jim said, folding his arms and sighing. 'All right.'

Frank looked off, left and right. He placed one hand on Jim's shoulder and pointed with the other hand.

'Right. Just keep an eye on those scaffold fittings down there for me, Jim,' he said. 'Some bastard's been having them away and I intend to find out who it is!'

ANDY'S EFFORT

Andy was making an effort, like the man from RELATE said they both had to. He cooked dinner and she wasn't happy about that. It was a dish he had experimented with. Maybe surprise each other, in small ways – the man had grinned in a cheesy way and spun slightly in his swivel chair as he spoke, smiling in her direction. Andy had taken a dislike to him. At that point. Having gone in with fairness in his mind. Why had they gone to see him? He was just a jumped-up somebody. A right Nonce doing a cushy job for a living. He didn't care in the slightest. Clock on, clock off. Waste of time, money and effort, in his – Andy's – opinion.

Fat smug bastard.

Maybe surprise each other in small ways. Take this lemon. Do you take this lemon? He had taken the recipe from a cookery book. It meant that he'd had to go out and buy a few extras; some herbs and a lemon. He'd bought a bottle of wine as well. It was fairly expensive but on Special Offer – so he had bought three. Well, it was recommended.

'Wine!' Paula exclaimed when she came in from her part-time job. Then sniffily: 'Won the lottery have we? Don't you realise that with you not having an income, money lies at the root of our problem?'

'It goes with the recipe!' He pointed to the book which lay open on the worktop.

'Even so…'

Andy took a deep breath. 'It goes with the recipe. Right?' He stared at her.

Paula took several deep breaths, counting them. She held up her palms. Andy looked elsewhere, shook his head.

They ate at the table in the kitchen. She could hardly bear to look at him – except to answer a direct question. Then it was a fleeting, vague response, usually sarcastic.

'How did your day go?'

She stared at him. 'How did yours!'

'I asked first!'

She shrugged. 'Can't talk, got my mouth full.'

She didn't even comment on the meal, just stuffed it in, ungraciously. It was times like this that he thought of other times. And their sex-life had reached this state. Small sighs and general weariness. A straightforward humpedy-humping session once a month – not even *that* some months. And then it was an effort. Ennui. He'd have to look that up. He knew the word and what it meant but he didn't know how to say it. Her eyes flicked round as she ate and drank; slurped – dwelt on the wall, the calendar, the ceiling. She sniffed, sniffed some more, pursed her lips, pouted, stuffed home food. Without finishing, she pushed the plate away; stood up, licked her lips – an awful smacking sound. Once those lips had been so important to him, their very being. He had longed for them. She picked up her glass of wine, walked through to the lounge and flopped down on the sofa. He watched her go, her hips and shoulders swinging with determined attitude. Once he had liked her determined attitude. Now it distressed him.

She watched telly, flicking through the channels again and again. He could hear her from the kitchen, looking for something banal and unchallenging. Her level, to luxuriate on, a melodrama or chat show. A sit-com. She clicked the telly off and it fell quiet. The house was quiet. He sat at the kitchen table sipping the white wine – which he found quite syrupy and not to his liking. But then he fetched another bottle from the fridge and popped the cork on that. He hoped that she heard the popping noise. The sound of someone Enjoying Themself.

There was another noise, a loud outburst, a wailing from upstairs. Jack. Jack cried and cried. He sat there, staring. He heard Paula get up from the sofa and trudge up the stairs, go into the room, lift Jack from his cot, cuddle and pacify him and come back down. Jack went quiet. All was quiet. Peace. Andy stood up. He started clearing the plates, carrying them across and stacking them in the dishwasher, as quietly as he could. He tiptoed and peered through the crack in the door, into the lounge.

Paula was sprawled in the armchair. She was watching the telly with the sound down. Her blouse was open. And there was Jack, at her breast – the lucky bastard!

––––––––––

16

THE ABSOLUTE BOTTOM LINE

Kev Plimsoll was sitting on his own on a stool in the saloon bar of The Grapes, where he preferred to sit, when he heard Jack, round the public, telling someone about Monty.

'Cunt could sell ice cream to an Eskimo!' Jack said, loudly, laughing, and all the others laughed too.

Kev grinned. He shook his head, sipped his pint, put down his glass and then shook his head again and smiled to himself. He smiled at the idea in his head in which he saw Monty leaning out the side of an ice cream van in some snowy part of Greenland, thick snow falling, handing a cornet with a chocolate flake sticking out to an Eskimo in a parka and taking the money, while a line of Eskimos – with those sort of tennis racquets on their feet – stood queuing.

That was Monty! Kev looked at the clock. He finished his beer. He had to get back to work.

He walked out of The Grapes, ten yards along the pavement, under the viaduct and turned right, up the hill towards 'Johnny Thompson's Furniture Warehouse'. Monty and Kev had a business on the side, buying and selling motors. They operated from a double garage which Monty sub-rented from someone who rented from the Council. It was illegal but nothing 'dodgy-illegal'. The garage was in a block of four rows on a forecourt behind 'Johnny Thompson's Furniture Warehouse' – which gave them the added advantage of an on-site phone through Jack, who worked in the warehouse accounts department.

What they'd do is buy up old bangers and wrecks, maybe from one of the county auctions, or privately – or even at times of desperation from Marsden and Son Ltd Car Spares (Breakers) – repair and respray them, add the cost of labour plus parts and a percentage profit, get an MOT ticket and sell through the small ads, a card in the post office window, word of mouth, or, back through the auction. It was easy as pie. The business fluctuated according to global economics, market forces and trends but ticked over more or less OK for a time. Kev (who had got the nickname Kev Plimsoll at school – where he had been hauled up before a whole school assembly for wearing plimsolls – which was all he had to wear because his family was poor) was a practical genius in the mechanical, electrical, panel-beating, welding and respray departments, while Monty handled the managerial/administration side.

They'd bought a van at an auction. It was yellow. A sort of powder-paint yellow. A Thames 7cwt that had been bodged up, filled here and there, and hand-painted. Despite the repaint,

17

Monty reckoned it was ex GPO – which was a selling point. At the auction Kev had propped up the bonnet, leaned in, stared at the engine and nodded slowly and that had been enough for Monty. Monty reckoned that Kev had an instinct the way that some people have for horses and Deke had with certain animate things. Two remould tyres and a new clutch cable, a new wing and a rub down and respray – making it less blatantly yellow – and Monty was confident of a healthy return. Having, as he explained to Kev, studied their marketing viability. Monty's acumen proved, as per normal, spot on. For, no sooner had Kev spent two days and three evenings, and much of three nights, getting the van primed and pristine, than Monty, through his network of business associates, had secured a prospective buyer: Mr G Bentley – Arthur from The Grapes' brother-in-law, a bricklayer who needed a van for work so that his wife could use the Toyota during the day for shopping and running the kids to school and back. That was the bottom line. As straight fifty-fifty splits went Monty envisaged this one as smooth as sandpaper.

Kev grinned and nodded, wiped his hand on the rag he was holding, noticed a smudge of polish on the wing of the van and bent over and rubbed it. He stepped back and straightened up and put the rag back in his overall trouser pocket. Then he said, 'Hang on?… Sandpaper ain't smooth!'

'Ah ha! That depends whether you're looking at it up close or far away!' Monty said, brightly.

Kev shook his head. He saw that queue of Eskimos again.

Come the day though, came the hitch. It was one of those rarities. An occasion when Monty's foresight, or insight, failed him. Of course, there was a female involved. Mr G Bentley was due at five pm. At three Monty and Kev had set the yellow van out on the centre of the forecourt, run the engine and buffed the bodywork to a sheen. It was an exceptionally hot day. The sun was pouring down and the light gave the yellow van an electric aura. It shimmered: 'Buy me, Buy me.' Kev felt a lump in his throat at that point, that he always felt on these occasions but didn't like to show – rather the way Monty could get about swine. They were standing back, pleased with their work, regarding their distorted reflections – hands in pockets, smiling – in the chrome bumper, when Jack came out of his office and strolling across the forecourt towards them, with a serious look on his face. He had a pen behind his ear, and he scratched his forehead as he walked. Monty heard him sigh loudly and looked round.

'What's up, Jack?' Monty said, light-heartedly. 'Your dog died?'

'Worse than that, Monty,' Jack said, frowning. 'It's Geraldine.' Jack sighed as he drew up. 'I'm afraid she's gone into labour.'

18

'What?'

''Fraid so. She's farrowing down. Looks to me like this Deke knows as much about pig farming as I know about nuclear thermodynamics!'

Monty shook his head. Jack chuckled. Kev stood there, arms folded, not knowing whether to look this way or that.

Jack said, 'Well...' and turned and began strolling back. 'I could try for that Bentley mush and cancel for you,' he called over his shoulder.

Monty looked at his watch and then at the van sat there shimmering yellow; pounds, shillings and pence. 'Nah,' he said. 'We'll sort it – but thanks all the same, Jack.'

Jack, without looking round, stuck up his hand and disappeared back in the warehouse.

Monty, stroking his chin, stared off after him. Jack had that walk of a person fully aware of their own importance. 'Cunt sometimes oversteps his authority,' Monty mumbled, referring to Jack's slight of Deke (who Monty, on the other hand, could and would slight like an old friend). He turned back, looked at Kev, then at the yellow van and then back at Kev. 'KEV!' he shouted, his face lighting up as if the spark of a new scheme had just, right that second, struck him.

Kev sat in the van, behind the wheel, in the driving seat, considering, hard. 'Hm,' he thought. Then a longer, 'Hmmm...' It was hot in the van. He was sweating. He wound down the window but it made a piercing, scraping noise where the inner mechanism was worn and stiff so he wound it up again – double quick. He opened the van door, climbed out and stood and leaned on the side of the van, rested his arms on the scorching roof and his head on his arms so that he was looking straight across towards a row of garage fronts and the viaduct beyond that and the mill chimney against the distant fields and open sky. He squinted with one eye and then the other.

'Two,' he mumbled to himself. 'Easy... as... pie'

Kev felt the sun on his bare shoulders. He had the top of his overall down, tied at the waist with the arms knotted at the front. He stood back, wiped his hand on a rag he pulled from his pocket. He looked at the van again and experienced a tingle of pleasure. He liked motors: lines, shapes, curves, grease, oil, spark-plugs, head-gaskets, rockerbox covers, valves, pumps, exhaust systems, wheel arches, hoses... as for this administration side of things though...

Monty had gone back to the farm. 'This one's as easy as pie, anyway,' he'd said, shrugging. 'A blind bloke could sell it to a deaf one, or the other way round!' Then he'd thought and coughed. 'Just don't go below two, that's the bottom line – the absolute bottom line. One thing that worries me about this Bentley – apart from him being Arthur's relation – he's a bricklayer, yeah? Money-grabbing bastards! They think they're it! Plus they're used to bartering prices – if you know what I mean.'

Kev hadn't known what he meant, but he had nodded. Now he shrugged and circled the van again, checking her over. He bit his lip and checked his watch. He felt parched. He re-checked his watch. It was four. Bentley was due in one hour. Kev felt a little bit bored. He liked to be doing something, fiddling with a carb or rubbing something down. He yawned. He thought about going to sleep but he was scared that if he went to sleep, say in the back of the van or across the seats of the Capri parked in the garage (their latest acquisition), like he usually would when he felt tired, he mightn't wake up again for a day and a half (this had happened once, on a Wednesday – he'd woken up on a Friday, just in time for lunch). Monty might not be too pleased if he missed this Mr Bentley. Kev walked across the forecourt to the garage anyway. Inside the garage, behind the Capri, keeping cool, there were a couple of quart bottles of cider Monty had brought up for later on. Kev went over and unscrewed the top and took a decent healthy swig. 'Two,' he said, screwing the cap back and smacking his lips together, 'Mister bricklayer Bentley!'

Monty was astute. He'd said to Kev, in a low voice (even though there'd been no one in earshot), 'The thing to do, the best way, like, is to start him up at... (Monty waggled his hand in the air)... say two forty-two fifty and then bring him down. Let him knock you down though. You know when you're fishing down the lakes and you get the fish on the line and then you let him have a little swim out and around to wear himself out before you pull him in?' Monty winked. 'That's the best thing, make him think he's doing it all himself. That's, sort of, psychology.'

Kev took what was left of the second bottle and went and sat down, just outside the garage, on the concrete. He started to feel sleepy. The sun blazed down and the sky and concrete buckled. His head dropped and rolled to his chest. His shoulders slumped. A car hooter bibbed somewhere and he stood up quickly and looked around. He checked his watch. Then he walked over to the standpipe at the far end of the forecourt, poured out water on to his hands and drenched his head and shoulders. He took a broom from the garage and swept their part of the forecourt and Mr Taylor's next to theirs and beyond, apart from old Jeffers' – who always moaned if they had the radio on – which he swept all the dust on to. He walked over and circled the van, taking the rag from his pocket and wiping off a couple of smudges as he went. Then he checked his watch again, sighed and went over, opened the door, let off the handbrake and pushed the Capri out on to the forecourt; pulled the catch and walked round, upped the bonnet and leaned and peered in.

Kev opened his eyes. His feet and legs felt warm but the top of him, where he'd stripped off the overall, felt cold. He stared straight up at bits of sky, past the fuel pump and alternator. He heard a cough. The bits of sky were blue blue. There was another cough and then another. A face suddenly appeared, peering down at him, through the engine. Kev started with shock and went to get up and hit his forehead on the bottom of the starter motor and then banged the back of his head on the concrete. 'Bollocks!' he shouted.

'Er, hello?' the face said, cheerfully.

Kev slid out, stood up, smoothed his hair and then rubbed his head, back and front.

'About the van? Which is *that* one, I presume?'

'Uh huh.' Kev brushed himself down. He pushed over his hair and adjusted the overall where it had fallen down on his hips slightly. Geoff Bentley stepped aside and looked away, respectfully. He stood there with his hands in his pockets, looking towards the van, grinning.

'Warm day.'

'Uh huh.' Kev scratched his forehead and glanced and took in Bentley. He was wearing shorts, long baggy shorts; and a white polo shirt with the collar up. He jiggled jauntily. His hair was pushed back in a kind of quiff – Elvis-like. His face was brown leather, creased from too much sun, smiling – he looked like an Australian, or a golfer. He was short, stocky and friendly – suspicious, just as Monty had predicted.

'And they say it's gonna get warmer, there's a front moving up from the gulf.'

'Uh huh.' Kev looked away, felt in his pocket and brought out the rag and wiped his hands. He looked up the forecourt, over at the van and back towards 'Johnny Thompson's Furniture Warehouse'. Jack came walking out and stood there in the sun in his shirt-sleeves, sort of looking over. Kev raised his hand, as if to say: 'It's OK, Jack.' Bentley, hands in pockets looked round to see who Kev was waving to. Jack just stood there. 'Sometimes he sort of oversteps his... himself,' Kev explained.

'Right,' Bentley said. 'Know the type!'

'Oh yeah,' Kev said, self-assuredly.

They circled the van, three times. Kev followed, hands in pockets. He looked in the left back window when Bentley looked in the right. In there it was spotless and carpeted, Kev had seen to that himself. Bentley swaggering round with his hands in his pockets grunted approvingly and Kev acknowledged him. At one point he removed his hand from the pocket of his shorts and ran it along the roof slyly – which irritated Kev a bit, because he knew that he was checking to see if the van had been rolled; either that or he'd seen people do that before. After doing that Bentley walked round and stood at the front of the van, looking down. Kev flicked the catch and propped up the bonnet, then went and climbed in the van, checked for neutral and turned the ignition and the engine fired immediately, without choke. He left the engine ticking over and climbed out and went and stood next to Bentley.

'Nice vans, these.'

'Uh huh.' Kev wiped sweat from his brow. Bentley did the same and then, stepping back, brought out a pack of cigarettes. He took one, put it in his mouth and then held the open pack out to Kev. Kev shook his head, but he immediately felt bad about it, as if he might have caused offence. Even though he didn't smoke he thought maybe he should have taken one and put it behind his ear. The sun beat down. Kev looked up and down at the humming engine. Bentley lit up and swallowed and nodded approvingly. Kev put down the bonnet and went and turned off the engine. Bentley moved round so that they were opposite sides of the van, facing each other across the roof.

Bentley blew out smoke and grinned. 'Yeah, my brother had one of these, for years. Reliable! He wouldn't have nothing else for his business!' He paused, waiting, and then carried on. 'Had a contract-cleaning business at the abattoir – until the day he sliced his arm off that is!' He paused again. 'Yeah, it was on one of the machines.' Kev winced, shifted and wiped his brow. 'Didn't get a penny out of them! That's the worse thing. You hear of some people...' Bentley looked away from him and up at the sky, shook his head, frowned and then looked back across the van roof. 'He wasn't wearing a safety hat.' He dragged on his fag and blew out smoke. 'Can you believe that? It's what they said... Just below the elbow,' he continued, laying his arm on the roof and running his finger across to demonstrate. 'No safety hat! Eh? I mean, you hear of some people getting millions for repetitive strain injury. But, then, in this world you have to count your blessings. There's always someone worse off. Like people who can't get enough to eat. There's one person dies every four seconds from starvation!' Bentley fixed directly on Kev. Kev shifted from foot to foot and wiped his brow with his arm. He suddenly felt hungry and then guilty – thinking about the amount of food he'd consumed that morning even: double bifta and chips at 'Betty's Blue And White Cafe'.

'What you asking?' Bentley said suddenly, dropping his voice.
'Er...' Kev started. He stood up and stepped back, put his hand in his pocket and felt the rag.
Bentley rubbed his eye. 'I'll be honest with you. I did have a peek at the book price this afternoon and I've noticed that there are quite a few of these on the market, in the trade papers I mean. I've got an in-law who knows someone who works for Simmonds, yeah?' Bentley laughed and pointed across the van, straight at Kev. 'So you can't tuck me up, mister!' He laughed, a huge laugh. Kev shrugged and laughed too.

Bentley disappeared, ducked down suddenly, out of sight. His voice continued, muffled. 'I noticed some rust bubbles under these wheel arches, for instance...' He popped up again, smiling broadly, 'But... I suppose I'm willing to go to...' He shrugged, paused and screwed up his face. 'Say, two two 0? Two twenty?... Used notes?'

Kev felt the heat beating down. He looked away, towards 'Johnny Thompson's Furniture Warehouse'. Easy enough. Then a bell went off in his head. He thought of Monty and some important business Monty had left him to attend to; starving people, Eskimos, fishing. He thought and looked down at the dust on the concrete forecourt. Monty said, 'Let him swim out a bit, make him think he's doing it!' Kev scratched his head. Two hundred, he thought. The absolute bottom line!

The heat was unbearable. He felt sweat on his lip. A wasp came bothering and he waved his hand and shooed it away, again and again. All the time Bentley was looking at him, his eyes narrowed, studying.

'Or, two... thirty?' Bentley said. Kev looked at him. Bentley was still smiling, full beam. 'Got other parties interested, is it?'

Kev sighed. He grinned, shook his head and smiled back at Bentley – waiting for him to swim out. He leaned on the van roof, carefully so as not to smudge it, put his hand out over the roof, palm down, and waggled it – the way he'd seen Monty do loads of times. He cleared his throat. 'It ain't so much that.' He wiped sweat from his forehead. 'I've got a partner.'

Bentley carried on smiling. He nodded. 'Got you!' he said.

Kev nodded, a slow deliberate nod, and smiled back. Then there was a silence before Bentley said, quickly: 'Two and a half? I think that's my limit, though, cash wise.'

Kev grinned, stared at him and shook his head... 'Nope.'

'Nah?'

'Nope.' Kev waggled his hand.

Bentley shrugged. 'Two sixty on a cheque?'

Kev sighed, the heat seemed to be burning into his brain. He shook his head again, in disbelief. 'Now you're going the wrong way!'

'The wrong way?'

'Uh huh, see, you're going up instead of down!' He leaned off the van and stepped back. 'Maybe there's some stuff you don't know – like round the door seals where we've put in chicken wire and just filled it and painted over.' He shrugged. 'Not to mention the mileage clock – I mean to say... you know...' He trailed off. Bentley studied him again. Kev grinned.

Bentley frowned and then, slowly, his leather face creased to a grin. 'Ha ha. Ha ha ha.'

Kev grinned wider.

'I see. You're making me have it!' Bentley shook his head. He tutted. 'No, don't get me wrong now! I weren't casting aspersions on your integrity, pal.' Bentley paused and sighed. 'OK I won't insult you.' He paused, then said: 'All right, you win, two six five. On a cheque though.'

Kev suddenly felt the heat pressing down on him. The fish was swimming away and he felt overwhelming fatigue; dog-tired. 'Two hundred!' he blurted out. 'Two hundred! Take it or leave it! ...And that's the bottom line!'

Bentley sped off in the yellow van, full throttle, happy, smiling, waving an arm out of the window as he went. I should have told him about that window squeaking as well, Kev thought, waving after him. The van moved out of sight. Kev stopped waving and patted his bulging pocket.

Kev shut and put across the bar and double locked the garage. He walked across the sunlit forecourt, gently patting his pocket containing the two hundred smackers. Monty'd be pleased with this day's work. Chuffed; very pleased. Meanwhile, he needed to get down The Grapes, have a pint and a sit in the garden in the shade.

As he walked across Jack strolled out from his office, put up his thumb. 'I was keeping an eye there, Kev,' he said, hitching his trousers. 'Did it go as smooth as we thought it would?'

Kev smiled. 'Smooth as sandpaper!'

Jack watched him go down towards the viaduct, bouncing along, patting his pocket as he went. Jack shook his head.

JIM, MY EX-NEIGHBOUR

I was thinking about my ex-neighbour. Not the ex-neighbour that my wife ran off with. Or the ex-neighbour that my wife had a fight with (that was at the old address). I was thinking about my ex-neighbour to our left in Beech Road, Jim.

I liked Jim. He was a failure. An accomplished failure. His attitude to life was a shrug. He practised his shrug first thing in the morning out in the back yard after contemplating the prospect. He had two cardigans, blue and a lighter blue, and standing there, hands in his blue cardigan pockets he would take in the air and then, very slowly let out a couple of half-hearted sighs. It seemed that each day brought with it some new burden.

'You struggle against it with decreasing energy,' he said, hands in cardigan pockets, over the fence. 'Until one day you stop struggling and then you die.'

I liked Jim for the straightforward reason that I generally find people likeable or otherwise: because he conceded something. I never told Jim that I liked him of course, which I kind of regret now. And at first I never liked him at all. In fact at first I found him a pain in the arse.

We exchanged to Beech Road impressed by the garden and its potential as much as the house, and once we were more or less straightened out inside I set to work outside. This interested Jim because he had once been a keen gardener himself and then his wife had left him without so much as a hint that she was in any way dissatisfied with her lot and at a time when he believed that they were sailing along effortlessly, on a pleasant breeze, on an even keel, as he put it – cruising up the middle lane in overdrive.

'You don't get overdrive anymore, Jim. You get a fifth gear.'

'Is that so?' Jim said, slightly irritated. He didn't drive any more on doctor's advice. He looked away left, towards some drooping old elms that stood in a small wood beyond the fence at the end of the garden, maintaining fascination for about one second and then relaxing. 'I used to have overdrive on my Wolseley, six-cylinder. In a way, I suppose, that was the beginning of the end. Those Sunday afternoon drives. June got to staring out the window and fidgeting. Seeing how the other seven-eighths lived.' Jim laughed his dry, hollow laugh.

After his wife, June, left – with the kids, Sandra and Neil – Jim carried on stoically. And I suppose that it would be true to say that at that point Jim was a stoic in the original, philosophical sense of the word and that that degenerated into cynicism, but again in keeping with its original sense. His stoicism was due, to a degree, to the advice of his doctor, Doctor Ted Harris, who was the area

GP for years until growing unease about his competence led to an unceremonious, hush-hush retirement. The practice was succeeded by a partnership that included Doctor Trendy (well – that's what he came to be known as) a youthful bearded energetic rugger-swilling amateur dramatic type, who seemed convinced that sex lay behind everything. Jane Carter, a young newly-wed from the other end of Beech Road, went to him complaining of a persistent sore throat and Doctor Trendy asked her straight out if she practised oral sex. That story buzzed through the village for a while and sort of heralded Doctor Trendy's tenure.

Jim went to see Doctor Harris after he fell out of a tree and broke his arm. Two days after. Doctor Harris, who had had regular consultations with the then not-long-departed June, diagnosed Jim's broken arm as a sprain and told him that he was run down, but assured him that if he carried on stoically June would probably return, because he knew that she 'felt' for Jim and that she was merely suffering from a type of mid-life restlessness and confusion of identity that affected women in general.

'I can assure you, Mr...' He looked at his notes. 'Mr Valhela. My wife for instance...' Doctor Harris got up and strolled across to the window of his surgery and stood staring out with his hands clasped behind his back.

For a while Jim didn't say anything. Then he said, 'What, she left you, Doctor Harris?' (Jim thought that he and Doctor Harris were about to engage in one of those intimate self-revelatory doctor-patient discourses, such as you get on the box.)

'No, she went and signed up for an Open University course.' Doctor Harris stayed staring absently out of the window, while Jim, rubbing his 'sprained' arm sat looking at the cluttered desk and at the telephone and at a wall chart – a cross-section diagram showing the circulation of the blood stream.

'Fascinating all that,' he said to me, over the fence, while I was setting out, with sticks, string and a measuring rod, a herbaceous border.

'Hmm...' I said.

'Blood,' Jim said, looking down at the sticks and string and measuring rod. 'Hmm...'

I detected something in his tone. 'Well, you've got to use these,' I said. 'This setting out is the most important part.' Jim took his hands out of his pockets and held up two flat palms in a defensive gesture.

Doctor Harris, whose time was nearly up, having a stab at modern methods that were alien to him, still standing at the window, cleared his throat. 'How was sex between you and Mrs Valhela, Mr Valhela?'

'Laugh? I nearly pissed myself!' Jim told me. This was years later when his marital breakdown was all water under the bridge.

'Well, it was, is, a valid question,' I said, patting down the soil around the roots of some of these things I had stuck in the ground. I had got them from a catalogue, following up an advertisement in a magazine and I had felt really disappointed when they'd arrived. I straightened up, holding my back like gardeners do.

'Hmm...' Jim said, dismissing Freud in about quarter of a second. 'I thought about it after,' he said. 'He must have asked her the self-same question. He could have got it from her.' I was mildly surprised by Jim's naïvety here.

'Er, not necessarily, Jim.' I scratched my head and shot a glance towards our kitchen window where Sue, who was one of those people who was bored most of the time, sometimes stood earwigging.

June never did move back to 4 Beech Road, although Neil did – briefly. He turned up and hugged his natural father, moved himself in and nearly drove Jim bonkers.

'An 'ippy! A bloody 'ippy!' Jim said.

Neil was going through a Gestalt phase and he explained to Jim, in the nicest possible way, that he needed to kill him – metaphorically. Jim had learned to distrust metaphor – he was more of a concrete type. Neil was restless anyway and one day he hugged Jim and moved out again. He subsequently became a chartered accountant and a freemason, which Jim found doubly indigestible.

'I wanted him to have an honest trade, like me.'

'Well, they do a lot for charity,' I said.

'What, accountants?' Jim said, with a twinkle in his eye.

I found out, through Sue, who loved idle gossip, who June was. She lived on the main road, less than half a mile away, with her second husband, Alec Vine, the comparatively well-off owner-proprietor of Vine Mo Co where June had worked as a secretary at the time she had left Beech Road. I knew both Vines to say hello to from the garage and they were always friendly, polite and helpful and, as far as I could tell, as normal as normal people can be. Their middle-size bungalow next to the garage and the front garden was well-tended and not given to overstatement. I had no reason to dislike either Vine apart from a sneaking suspicion that neither seemed the type to concede that their life had been anything but thoroughly worthwhile. They drove a modern car each and they owned a share in a time-share apartment in Fuengerola. Their step-daughter worked for the social services and their step-son was an accountant and an active freemason. But now, after signing my Access receipt, as either of them twisted the card in their hand, going through the motions of checking the signature, I looked more intently for the faded distant look in their eyes, the give-away; some depth, or a hint of weariness; a momentary betrayal of guilt or confession of anxiety, restlessness; anything, anything!

Jim said, knowing and meaningfully, over the fence, that during the early days of his marriage he used to spend a lot of time – when he wasn't at work – gardening and doing bits and bobs, odds and sods, around the house, because he thought that that was what was expected of him. And when she left, following Doctor Harris's advice, he carried on that way.

'It is my experience in these cases,' Doctor Harris had said, pompously ('Never mind my 'king arm',' Jim said, interrupting himself). 'That nine times out of ten...'

'His experience?' Jim said. 'With a house up in Spring Vale, you know, up by the golf course, and a Rover V8 and a wife on the Open University!'

'She was only bettering herself, Jim,' I said, raking an area to a fine tilth before I put the lines across for a level, prior to turfing. I think Jim wondered who I meant, June or Doctor Harris's other half. But he went 'Bah!' anyway.

One day during this period; just after June had left, Jim came in from work (He had driven the crop sprayer until that stuff started getting on his chest and he was advised to give it up by Doctor H. – 'Oh, give it up! Just like that!' Jim said. Following that, he had found employment in the cricket ball factory. 'Great for your insides, I'm sure!' Although it did suit him, being a gentle stroll down the road and a gentle stroll back up; afternoon or evening – depending on the shift). He ate his lonely tea, watched the news, put on his gardening boots and walked out of the back door, down the steps into the yard (Jim always went through things that I thought were irrelevant to the plot in tortuous detail) and stood and surveyed things as they stood, an act that was always stage one of the stoic ritual.

'I remember it because the rooks were cawing,' he said. 'And, there was a fresh wind, coming from the east.' (I looked at him.) After that he walked over to the shed, paused, considered, looked at the garden again, opened the shed door...

He rubbed his chin. 'I remember saying to myself,' he said, staring down the garden, towards the elms, one of which he had once mysteriously fallen out of. 'Even if you do just an hour Jim – see, I was talking to myself! – to maintain the momentum. Knowing full well that momentum once lost is impossible to recoup...'

He trailed off. I looked at him again. He was still staring off.

But he didn't. He went back indoors, washed at the sink, shaved, cleaned his teeth, plastered down his hair, put on a white shirt and his best, charcoal grey, Italian style, suit and went to town.

'Literally... Chatham.'

'Chatham?'

'Yes. Chatham.' Jim crouched and did a half spin of The Twist fists in the air. 'Always been a bit of a mover on the floor. That's how I met June in the first place – she thought I had it!'

'How d'you get there? In the Wolseley?'

'Nah, train. I had given up driving at that point, doctor's advice. I turned to drink. Had a great time. Didn't know where I was or who I was. I ended up at a dance. And I pulled! Nice blonde bint in a frock. You wouldn't remember frocks, or bints. I was more of a classical mover, you know? Come Dancing, the fox-trot. She came from Strood. Only trouble was she was with someone and he started. He started it. The next week, because this dance, in some hotel – I forget the name of the joint – was a weekly affair with a resident band. I went back again. They wouldn't allow me in at first. I had to bribe the bouncer and he insisted on 'a drink' for his mate. This time she was there on her own, or with a girl friend. Anyway, to cut a long story short (Jim had never done that before, in my experience), I had a little spate of that; going out, drinking, smoking, living it up to the hilt.' He put his fists up again and did another half twist. 'And then one night I was standing there, up at the bar, in Chatham, all dressed up, charged up and raring to go, when suddenly I came over all blue and mellow. Strangest thing. And it was a sadness that I couldn't odds, drink as I might, dance as I might, with who I would. "What's up with you tonight, Charlie boy?" This Janey said to me. "You don't seem yourself."' (I looked at him, questioningly – he shrugged, embarrassed.) 'I was known as Charlie... in Chatham. Anyway, I hung around but I couldn't shake it. It was as if God was saying, "All right, Jim. You've had your fun but now you're just going through the motions. Quit, before you just become a sad parody of yourself."'

I looked at Jim. I think that he thought that he'd shot off at the mouth a bit so I didn't say anything. He shrugged and looked at the sky. 'They give rain tomorrow, on The Weather,' he said, reverting to his normal, matter of fact voice.

Jim told me all this and more as he, hands in pockets, followed me up and down the back and front garden, although staying his side of the fence and leaning and talking over it. The low chestnut-pole fence ran between the two gardens. On Jim's side there was a path of paving slabs which he had laid himself in what he called the summer of his content. 'Before the winter, see,' he said, looking at me to see if I'd got it, as if I was thicko or something. Now there were weeds growing up between the paving slabs. In fact Jim's garden was a bit of an eyesore. I felt sorry for him. When we'd viewed the house – with a view to exchanging – I'd remarked to

Sue that one of the first things I planned to do was get rid of that scruffy little fence and put up something decent, like the smart six-foot panel fence of our neighbour on the other side. There was an ulterior motive for that plan. Sue was a sun-worshipper and she would have no reservations about stripping off and lying there on her sunlounger in her bra and knickers. I never did put up the six-foot panel fence as I'd planned though. Out of respect for Jim's feelings. I felt that he would have taken it as an affront.

That turned out to be one of the hottest summers on record and without the high fence I wasn't over-enthusiastic about Sue sunbathing in her underwear. But she scoffed at that and pointed out, with some justification, that it was no different from a lot of the bikinis that anybody could view quite freely at any beach or public swimming pool. Sue had a point there, except that in fact there is a basic qualitative difference for most people between the concepts signified by the words bikini and underwear.

Jim, I think, was quite embarrassed by this indiscretion of Sue's at first and it even kept him away from the fence for a while. Then he went through a phase where he seemed intrigued. And then amused. Eventually he appeared to shrug it off and assimilate into his general overview and he carried on as before, apparently oblivious. I say, oblivious, but I now have reason, upon consideration, to believe that it may have caused some stirring in the depth of his soul.

And then me and Jim fell out – had the argument. It was a stupid disagreement that, like most differences with neighbours, started over something small and blew up out of proportion. It started, in fact, when I, impulsively, acting completely out of character, bought Jim a present. A Christmas present. This bloke came round the sites flogging cheap gear and I bought Jim a tie and matching umbrella. Even Sue thought I was mad. 'What's that miserable old git want a tie and an umbrella for?' was her contribution.

'To wear with a shirt and to keep his head dry!' was my reply. Sue tutted, shook her head in an exaggerated way, stared off and chewed her nails.

I waited to receive Jim's warm thanks. It got round to February. I was wandering round the back garden looking at things when Jim came sloping round and along the path at the side of his place. He was on his way back from work, early shift. It had been raining, though lightly, but enough so that his head was glistening and he was sniffling.

'Bloody poxy weather,' he whinged.

I'd been having a few problems of my own at that point and I just blew. 'Well why don't you use your new umbrella!' I shouted.

'Oh yeah, about that,' he said. 'What d'you think, I'm a scruffy bastard or what? Tell you what, your money would be better spent buying your wife some clothes to cover up and, since we're on the subject, maybe you should be keeping a bit more of an eye on things in that department, instead of poncing about in the garden trying to be... (he paused, deliberating)... middle-class!'

'What's that supposed to mean?' I said.

'It's supposed to mean what it means,' Jim said, huffily, coming right up to and almost coming over MY fence.

'And, come to that,' I shouted, 'how did you come to fall out of that tree. Eh? Your wife left you because you're a miserable loser and I reckon you got pissed and was trying to top yourself!'

Next morning I found the tie and umbrella, badly rewrapped, lying in our garden.

When my wife left I started to drink and hang around old haunts; pubs and clubs I had known previously. I even looked up some old friends, a lot of whom were sympathetic but... It was some time after. I hadn't spoken to Jim since that day and of course I haven't still and probably never will. One evening, after the drink and clubs phase, at about midnight as I lay awake thinking, I heard a noise outside, like low muffled sounds. Maybe a voice. Singing? Foxes? Foxes, I decided. I had put out the bin bags and, thinking about the foxes and how they would sometimes raid the bags, I climbed out of bed and went to the window. It was a clear starry night and from the main bedroom window there was a view of the estate in its hollow and the valley and the hills beyond and I stood there for a while just looking. It was then, in the moonlight, that I saw the strangest sight and, what I realised was the probable cause of the noise I'd heard – it was that old fool from next door drunk and waltzing round his front lawn in his blue cardigan with a whisky bottle for a partner.

SCHIZO JOHN AND AL

There was a daily job of loading a trailer, a long flat-back that was positioned by the brick stack in the compound each morning before we arrived at half seven. The trailer took about forty thousand bricks, plain flettons. As well as loading that, in between we were responsible for unloading any lorry that turned up on site: bricks, breeze-blocks, cement, pipes and collars, manhole covers, roof tiles, plasterboard, window and door frames, bathroom suites... By 'we' I mean, me, the ganger – Bill Hawkins, John 2, Bald Ken, Eugene, Wurzel, Leo, George, Henry, Roy, Dave the Sailor and Al and Duncan: a pair of students.

That was at the beginning. Then the mornings were cold with a hard frost. Usually though when you got a frost, by eleven the sky was clear and it turned out a warm sunny day.

In time, the boss, Schizo John, whittled the gang down, creaming off the more talented – those that could lay drains, services, sets, kerbs or concrete; shutter, or drive dumpers or tractors. The basic loading/unloading gang was reduced to me and Roy, the ganger-man Bill Hawkins, and the two students, Al and Duncan. A couple of the others would return to pitch in if we became really over-stretched.

One of the students, Al, had long hair and a beard, as you'd expect a student to have, and a certain way of speaking that was both defensive – of his being a student and insufferably pompous. He would say things like – if say John 2 said to him, 'Had it lately?' – 'Made love you mean? It is a beautiful and rewarding experience and all about experience in the original French meaning of the verb which is closer to our own "experiment", and, though I am no expert, I do try to improve my technique through a frank uninhibited discourse with whomsoever my partner may be.'

Or, on religion: 'I don't know about God because I haven't properly thought that through. Mhm? I believe that Jesus definitely existed, in the mortal sense, although I think that his philosophy has been expropriated and that he was more likely what we would now classify as radical left wing, à la Wedgie Benn!'

All this while we were bent double loading bricks on the trailer or humping ten ton of cement into a shed. What a prat, a smug prat!

Schizo John liked Al. Al amused him. Plus Schizo admired his Teflon-like resilience. I mean, being a student and worse still looking the part, made Al a butt from the off. But when Schizo John'd have a jovial laugh with the lads from the concrete gang at Al's expense, Al would come back with: 'Ha ha, aren't you funny. Eh! I'll get you a false nose and glasses and a paper hat!'

Al was short-sighted and he went round squinting rather than wear his glasses and risk further ridicule. So Schizo John – irrationally to us but true to form – made him the tractor driver and then went absolutely berserk when Al reversed and put the trailer down a soakaway excavation. Berserk John, as opposed to his alter ego Jovial John, sacked Al on the spot, but later Jovial John relented, had a chat about it with Berserk John who rejoined with the now legendary remark 'No. It's not your fault, son. It's mine. I should never have employed you in the first place!' and persuaded himself to reinstate Al, but gave him the worst job on site, ever: tea-boy.

One day Al the tea-boy lit the gas oven, using the automatic switch, to heat some meat pies the bricklayers had bought in. But he couldn't work out if the oven was alight or not, So, being a clever bastard student, he lit a match and peered inside and in the subsequent explosion singed his hair, beard and eyebrows. Black faced and in shock Al staggered out of the tea hut and ran screaming down the road to where Schizo John and some of the others were finishing off a block of garage bases. Schizo John, who liked to finish off garage bases with the lightest of tamps, was in a jovial mood and the sight of Al at this point added to that. John burst out laughing, even when Al tripped and fell head-first in the freshly-laid concrete, and the concrete gang followed suit.

'Ha ha, you're so funny!' Al shouted. 'I'll get you all false noses and paper hats!' And he stormed off in a huff.

About one hour later a large green new registration Volvo drew up on site and a large blue-rinse haired woman, Al's mum it turned out, jumped out of the car, leaving the driver's door swinging, and proceeded to lay into the entire concrete gang, verbally and no holds barred. She threatened to have every one arrested, to fight, and to sue Schizo John – who she called 'mad' – and the main contractors, for whom a near relatives of hers worked – for every penny they had, for 'non-observance of proper safety regulations'.

'And my brother-in-law just happens to be a London barrister,' she shouted as she climbed back into the new reg. green car. 'A QC!' Then she paused and stared round at everyone. 'So, I think a few of you have got an almighty shock coming to you! One thing that is for sure, not one of you has heard the last of this!'

And that was the last anybody heard of that.

———————

SUMMER LIGHTNING

I was belting down the track. I heard the sound of a motor coming up behind me. I moved over. But then there's this loud: bib-bib! bib-bib! bib! bib! A dark-green Range Rover came up alongside me, so close that the wing mirror clipped my right arm. I nearly lost my balance and entered up in the hedge. I must have hovered that way, because, next thing, I heard the sound of someone laughing. I looked over. It was Smiffy, Jim Smith. He was hoeing his vegetable plot and the sound of the hooting had made him look up. Now he came up to his back gate and leaned on it and chortled some more.

'What you laughing at?' I braked, swung off the bike and wheeled it over.

'You!' he shouted, grinning all over his face.

He stood there. I stopped, leaned over the bike and brought my tobacco tin out from my jacket pocket.

'Who's that then?' I looked down the track in the direction the Range Rover had taken.

'That's him, the new bloke at Tynans.' Jim looked left and right and then leaned over the gate towards me, dropped his voice to a whisper. 'Apparently, she's quite tasty. Used to be on the telly and that.'

'Is that right,' I said licking down the paper. I offered Jim the tin. He shook his head.

'Given it up!' he said, stepping back and folding his arms tight.

'Is that right,' I said, looking back up the track towards Tynans.

The track was a short cut from Green Lane to the hill that led down to the village. From where I worked on Hobsbawm's farm it was easier for me to cut straight through the woods – the coppice where they grew the trees for chestnut fencing – and then down the long slope that led through another small woods and came out on the track. The track finished, trailed off to a narrow path there. Although, further up, if you beat through the brambles, you'd find the remains of a barn that had fallen into disrepair. Directly to the left as you came out of the woods, lying back and set in its own grounds, stood a big white house that had forever been known as Tynans, even though there was a sign at the entrance to the drive that said Woodstock Place. There were apparently nine bedrooms in the house and two bathrooms. In the grounds there were stables and, at the bottom of the back garden, a proper tennis court. From the rear you had a view of hop gardens and rows of orchards, woods, and open fields stretching down the side of the valley and out over the weald. As you went by Tynans the track ran for about a mile, with woods and orchards either side. Then you came to the row of converted hop pickers' cottages that backed on to the track.

It was my wife, that evening, who reminded me of the incident.

'Apparently the wife of the man who's taken Tynans used to be on the telly and that. I hadn't heard of her myself.'

I was reading the paper. I read to the bottom of the page. Then I lowered the paper, picked up my cup and took a sip of tea.

'What was she in then?'

'Just adverts and that, mainly.'

'What adverts?'

'Meat. I think.'

That night when I took the dog out for her late piss I walked up the track. I brought out my tobacco and rolled a fag while the dog rummaged round, up the bank and in the woods. I looked across the hedge at Tynans. The curtains were drawn except for the top dormer windows. Several lights were on. An outside light, fixed to the side of the house, shone over the bottom end of their drive. The Range Rover wasn't there.

In the morning when I rode by at half past five, on my way to work, the house was in a glistening mist where the day was just coming to light. The Range Rover was there in the drive but its bonnet was more or less dry, so I guessed that it hadn't been there that long. I left my bike, nipped along the drive, knelt beside the Range Rover, stuck a matchstick in the valve and let down the tyre.

My wife looked at me in that way, busting to come out with something. Finally she said, 'She had a nervous breakdown.'

I looked at her and then back at the telly and then back at her. 'Who?'

'That woman. The one at Tynans I was telling you about. She used to be on a game show as well. Jane told me. Her Tina has got the cleaning job that she had with the last people, the Royle-Jones. The woman told her herself. Just came out with it while they were having a conversation. "A few years ago I had a nervous break-down." Bold as brass.' She sniffed and folded her arms and stared at the telly.

I brought out my tobacco tin. I looked at her. 'I thought you said she was in the adverts?'

'She was,' she said, still looking at the telly. 'Meat. And game shows as well.' She paused. 'Do you remember Friday Postbox? Where you could win a weekend break for two?'

'No?'

'Your memory. It's like a sieve!'

I stared at the telly. In fact I did remember the programme. Way back. The girl in the black dress with long wavy hair and a big smile who came down the steps at the end every week carrying the transparent globe that was full of viewers' postcards. Then they'd pick out a winner.

'I don't know why people have to make it their business anyway,' I said. 'See. That's the trouble round here – everyone wants to know what everyone else is up to. That Smiffy, he's the same.'

'Huh,' she went.

In the morning when I rode up the track the porch light was still on. The Range Rover wasn't there.

Jim Smith was right about one thing. I found that out when I nearly came a cropper for the second time on account of that household.

I was on my way home, travelling fairly fast. I came down the slope and off the bank and hurtled out of the woods on to the track, same as usual. She was cutting back the rose bushes that overhung their front hedge. I suppose I frightened her.

'Oh my God!' she gasped as I flew out. She jumped out of the way and that put me off and I turned and skidded, spraying up mud and gravel but managing to avoid her. A golden retriever standing at the entrance to their drive jumped up barking. The shears clattered to the ground. She threw up her arms.

'It's all right!' I shouted back, to calm her down. She must have seen me wobble and nearly lose it. I heard her gasp and then she started to laugh. Then, because I needed to regain balance, I had to pedal as hard as I could. 'It's all right!' I shouted back again, glancing once over my shoulder as I rode away. She was standing there, smiling and looking after me and I could feel myself reddening up. I don't know why.

'And chocolate bars,' my wife said. 'Choc-Chip? Choc-Chip, Choc-Chip. Save some for me Mum!… Remember? The little kid with the cheeky grin? She played the kid's mum. In fact the more I think about it now, the more I'm sure I do remember her. She's kept some of her looks. She was down the post office this morning, buying a stamp.' She shrugged. 'Seems friendly enough. Must be hard when you lose your grip on reality. But then that's often the case with those type of people. I wonder if that's why there's no kids? Perhaps she couldn't have children. Perhaps that's what lies behind it all. Perhaps that's what lies behind a lot of things. It affects women.' She sighed. 'Things that we tend to take for granted, in normal circumstances.' She said all this as she was doing her ironing, looking down, nattering away to the ironing board.

'What are you on about?' I said. 'I don't know why you have to keep going on and on and on about it. Perhaps you haven't got enough to keep your mind occupied all day!'

'Huh! She picked up a pile of ironing and stomped out. I

grinned to myself, shook my head. Then I got up and took the dog out for a walk.

I was ploughing up on the top field. I saw her ride across the field below. A couple of times I had seen her, out riding on the bridle-path or crossing the lower field with her dog in tow. She trotted across the field and out of sight.

I was about to turn at the edge of the field when one of Lord Riley's pheasants poked its head out of a hawthorn bush, came out and strolled along, casual as anything, in front of me. Some-body's dinner! I thought, bringing the tractor to a slow halt. I leaned back and grabbed the pick handle that I keep in the cab for such occasions. Lord Riley's birds, being pen-reared for shoots, are so obliging they'll practically lay their neck on the ground and smile at you while you bash them one. Not that we were supposed to touch them. But if you accidentally ran one over... say, you couldn't help that! Besides, those old dodders were so pissed by the time they got to the shoot they couldn't hit my arse if it was painted bright yellow!

I climbed slowly out of the cab and moved carefully round the hedge side, gripping the pick handle ready. The bird stood there, preening itself in the sun. I moved beside it, lifted the pick handle... But, then, there was this sudden rustling noise behind me. The bird cocked its head, strutted a few paces and then flew up, startled. The yellow dog came bounding out from the woods and took off after it.

'Jesus!' I said, throwing down the pick handle.

'Hello.'

I turned round. She was there in a gap in the hedge up on the horse. She was smiling. She clicked her heels and came forward. I stroked the horse on the neck.

'You're the man on the bike who arrives out of nowhere,' she said, looking down at me, still smiling.

I walked over and picked up the pick handle. 'I was just about to bag a pheasant for dinner,' I said. I walked across to the tractor. I expected her to ride off but she dismounted, patted the horse and walked over behind me. The horse stayed still, flicked his head and snorted thick breath into the air. Walking towards the tractor, I noticed a small white fleck in the wall of the back tyre. I leaned in to take a closer look. From a distance I thought it could have been a split in the rubber.

I could feel her standing quite close behind me. The horse snorted again. 'Just checking this tyre,' I said. I glanced over my shoulder.

'Aren't they massive things.'

I stood up and turned and faced her. 'They cost about eighty quid a time those do,' I said.

What struck me was how small she was. Five foot four, or five, if that. She was wearing riding boots. Her hair was completely different – short, in a kind of bob. She was still smiling. She had a black jumper on and light coloured jeans. She looked off right, at the ridge and across at the lower field, where I'd seen her cut across earlier. I looked where she looked but there wasn't much to see, except a wide sloping, ploughed, flint-speckled field. A few rooks that had followed the tractor were walking round, pecking in the newly turned furrows. For the rest it was open sky, fields and woods. The top field was so called because it was situated at a high point on the side of the valley. It sloped gradually down to a small dell, and past that there were more fields and woods in the other direction.

'Charles Dickens used to live near here,' I said. 'Years ago. What do you think of it? Living here? Not that much doing is there?'

She slid her free hand in her front pocket and sort of hunched her shoulders. The yellow dog came back, panting. She took out her hand and leaned to stroke him. 'We love it. Don't we George?' The dog had returned minus the cock pheasant. Not much of a retriever, I thought, if he can't even catch a Riley pheasant.

'We had better let you get on with your work,' she said. She pulled down the sleeves of her jumper.

I shrugged. 'It's all right. I think I'm due a break. Should be finished by this evening I reckon.' I scratched my forehead and folded my arms. I looked at the dog which was panting like mad. She was looking around again, that light smile on her face. Despite the sun it was a fairly crisp day. 'You don't find it a bit boring then?'

'Not at all,' she said, brushing hair off her forehead. She looked at me. I felt myself going red.

'I remember you. Well, my wife does more... Off the telly. Choc-Chip, Choc-Chip. Save some for me, Mum! They'll probably ask you to cut the ribbon at the fete this year. They like to get a celebrity. One year they had that one from Crackerjack.'

She laughed. 'I don't know about that,' she said. She looked away again, squinting into the light. The sun lit on her hair. I thought that she had coloured up slightly.

I leaned back on the side of the wheel and brought my tin out of my top pocket. I got out a paper and started to roll a fag. The dog, George, had walked off and was sniffing round the hedgerow at the edge of the field. The horse took a couple of paces after him.

'D'you want one of these?' I said, licking down the paper.

'No thanks,' she said, smiling. 'I used to smoke though. Even those sometimes.'

'I can't smoke those other things. I had a cigar one Christmas. A few years back. A King Edward. Mind you, it's bad for your health... I've got some tea in a flask in the cab,' I nodded to my right. 'If you fancy a cup?'

'It really is sweet of you,' she said. 'But I'm fine thank you.'

I lit up the fag.

She looked away again, still smiling. Then, looking back at me, she said, 'Have you always lived in the village?'

'Yes. Yes. I have actually.' I felt myself flush red, for some reason. I dragged on the fag and scratched my forehead. I remembered a time when I had had a chance to move and work somewhere else, in another county. I thought, then I said: 'Well, that's not strictly true actually. For a time I lived in the next village down the valley. Except I was just a baby, too young to remember.' I wished I hadn't said 'baby' because she looked down at that point.

She bent down and picked up a flint. She held it out in front of her.

'These are wonderful.'

'Well, I'm not so sure about that.'

'Do they grow?'

'Do they grow? I don't think so,' I said, laughing.

'Well, where do they come from?'

I shrugged. 'Out of the ground.'

'Well, how do you know that they don't grow?'

I laughed again. 'Bloody nuisance, I know that. Get one of those jabbing into your tyre and that's it!'

Just after that she pulled the horse over, swung herself up and then smiled and waved and rode off. George followed. I used to see her quite often after that. She'd always stop for a chat but she'd never accept a cup of tea from the flask or anything. Carol her name was. Dean in the time that she was famous and then Henderson.

A path led off the track and ran through the woods and along the side of the orchard that lay across the back of Tynans. I took the dog out there one Sunday afternoon and went round checking on some nets and snares that I had set up here and there. I checked the nets and then whistled the dog and went walking on.

I had noticed a lot of cars crammed in the drive at Tynans and spilling back out on to the track the day before – so I guessed that there'd been some kind of function. Going along the orchard path you had a view of the back garden. I sat down on the low bough of a tree, keeping my feet on the ground. The dog came back and lay on the ground next to me. I brought my tin out of my pocket and rolled a cigarette. It was a pleasant, sunny day. I was wearing just a shirt and a pair of jeans.

The tennis court was at the bottom of the garden, surrounded by a high green wire-net fence. From there the lawn sloped slowly up and banked up to a patio. The doors of the house were open and people were sitting on chairs on the patio. More people drifted up and down the garden and others played tennis in the court, dressed in proper white tennis gear. You could hear the cluck of the ball going forward and back, forward and back, forward and back. A man was sat up in the proper high umpire's chair. He was dressed in a black jacket, with his shirt collar open and a loosened bow-tie, and he was holding a glass in one hand. Occasionally, jokingly, he would call out the wrong score and the players would laugh and stand and shout, hands on hips or waving their racquets at him, complaining in the same joking tone. The people up on the patio, meanwhile, just sat around talking. Then, one of them would stand up, go into the house, and come out again carrying a tray of drinks and take the tray round to each person, offering them a drink. When the tray was empty, apart from one drink, his own – the man would bow slightly, and the others would laugh. Then he would put the tray on the table and take his own drink and sit down again.

It was dry and dusty. I spat. I rolled up my sleeves and sat back on the bough. The dog lay down – although she looked up at me now and then, as if to say: 'Come on then? What's the point of just sitting here?'

I looked up at the blue sky and the sun about to go down. I sat and smoked another fag. I looked over. Now and then someone would rise from their seat on the patio and, glass in hand, walk down the steps and stroll down the lawn to the court and stand at the fence, watch the tennis for a while, and laugh at the antics of the drunken umpire and the other players. Then they would check their glass, notice that it was empty and stroll back up the lawn – maybe stopping on the way to look at the roses on the border, study the white flowers on the trellis or stop to chat with someone or, perhaps two or three people who happened to be strolling in the opposite direction. Once I saw the dog, George, walk halfway down the garden and then turn and walk back up again.

I didn't see her, or rather I couldn't make her out, until it had started to get dark. The tennis players had packed up and gone back up to the house. Then, after a while, some floodlights were switched on around the patio and three men and a woman in formal evening dress and carrying something, came out of the house and stood in a line on the right. The others sat down across the patio. After a pause the four in evening dress sat down, bent down and each picked up an instrument. Then they began to play. At first the sound was sharp and it jarred on your ears, but gradually, out of that, this pleasant, soft melody emerged. This went on for a while, one minute soft and then getting louder and then the sound would go way down low – a distant, sort of background rumble – while one of the violins played above them and, eventually, almost without you knowing it, the other instruments dropped away completely. It had turned fully dark by now and I had hardly noticed it. This thin, painful, wailing now seemed to have disassociated itself from the crowd on the patio and taken off, like a bird, rising, soaring into the black sky until it cut and then swirled and echoed off the hills and stretched and filled the valley. I looked up, almost expecting to see this black bird flying away. I felt something in my chest. I looked at the sky and all around and then back towards the house. The dog shifted near my feet. That's when I recognised her, because she must have stood up from her seat or, at that moment walked out from the house. She stood framed in the doorway with the light behind her. At that point I knew it was definitely her because the golden retriever, George, roused himself and went and stood next to her and she put down her hand and patted his head. She was wearing a long black dress, like the one she used to wear on Friday Postbox. She smiled around at everyone and, when she rubbed the tops of her arms someone stood up and handed her a jacket and she smiled and nodded and draped it over her shoulders. The musicians were playing a different tune now, more fiery. She walked out from the doorway, crossed the patio and, with the dog following, walked down the steps, out of the glare of the floodlights, to the garden. Then, with her arms folded and the jacket draped across her shoulders, she walked, slowly down in the direction of the tennis court.

The sky was deep black now and full of stars. The three-quarter moon hung above the ridge, through the trees in the woods beyond the top field, bright and clear. The air smelt of something sweet like apple blossom and this different music seemed to be seeping, slowly through the trees of the orchard and hanging like thickening mist. I watched her walk down the garden, now and then disappearing in some flickering shadow, and then emerging again in the light of the moon and the stars. She strolled down the lawn as far as the beech hedge, just before tennis court, that marked the border of the garden. Then she stopped and stood looking out, with her arms folded, staring out over the valley. George stood next to her, pointed up his nose and sniffed the air and I felt my dog shift again by my feet. She was standing there in the garden. Then she looked straight towards me. And that's when I had the sudden idea of calling out to her. I stood up and took a deep breath and opened my mouth and, yet, when I tried to speak, nothing came out. I saw her there, at the bottom of the garden, on the edge of the valley, looking out. The crowd up on the patio seemed lost, somehow immersed in the music that was swirling through the night sky. At one point, sure that she had seen me, I leaned right back in the shadow of the branches of the tree. She stood there for a while – exactly how long I couldn't say. She stood there looking out and then she shivered and, pulling the jacket tighter around her shoulders, she took one last look and then she turned and, with the dog following, walked slowly back up to the house.

———————

WAS THAT YOUR WIFE AND DAUGHTER?

There had been a shower of sleet earlier in the day but now the air was clear. Nick heard faint shouting as he crossed the main road from the bus stop. At one point he slid on the icy surface, staggered and straightened up. Traffic crawled in both directions. He threaded his way through the cars. The drivers tapped fingers on their steering wheels and stared out, grimly. Nick smiled to himself. He stepped up the kerb and hurried along the pavement, adjusting his shoulder bag as he walked. It was cold but he actually felt quite good; warm inside from having had a drink. It was early evening and darkening. He smoothed over his hair. The shouting grew louder. It came from the estate.

There had been tension again, lately. Since the campaign. This was the fifth flare-up and the culmination of the latest initiative. They had been advised as to these initiatives and their enactment – from the petitioning, letters to the press, to the seeing-it-through. This drive was called 'Let's Tidy Up Our Back Yard' (TUBY). It was happening on every estate in the borough. There had been TUBY leaflets, window stickers and badges, plus a financial incentive followed by a series of meetings; low-key, informal, relaxed empowerment meetings organised by the newly formed Estate Campaign Committee and the council Social Policy department. The first of these meetings Nick had enthusiastically attended. He had even, much to his own surprise, stood up and spoken. (Not without passion either – on the bin bags issue.) For a while he had sported a TUBY badge. He had intended to go to the second meeting but it had slipped his mind on the day. And he had given the third and each once since a miss. Not for any particular reason, and not because he was unsympathetic to the general cause. He was just sort of lazy when it came to things like that.

Nick walked on. The surge of spirits he'd felt gradually ebbing. The shouting grew louder as he neared the estate, a chorus of voices. There was a headiness in the sound and at one point he found himself speeding up. He slowed down. He sighed inwardly, felt a loose churning in his stomach. He had had five pints in the pub after work, which didn't help. And this, the shouting up ahead, was not the most heart-warming welcoming sound. But, then again, he understood the main point of view and some things were bound to give under the enactment of the initiatives. They had explained this at the first contact meeting, about 'pressure points' and 'give' and 'take'. 'Imagine a set of scales, yeah?' The TUBY man had said, holding out both palms. 'Call one "Give" and the other one "Take"... Hm?' 'The way these bin bags are allocated out is a disgrace,' Nick had said, falteringly, rising to his feet.

There had been murmurs of approval. People had looked on, admiringly. Nick felt queasy about the noise up ahead all the same. Even though it had nothing to do with him.

He had unconsciously speeded up again. He turned into the wider path that led on to the estate. The shouting continued, a sort of bawling, jarring the air, rising then falling. Nick sniffed, palmed over his hair and adjusted the bag on his shoulder. A ten foot brick wall stood either side of the path which carried on through an alley that ran beneath the flats to a large courtyard. The path was lit by swan-neck lamps. It was clean, even along the grass verges that used to be constantly littered with cans, bottles, wrappers, syringes, condoms. Nick had taken the odd leak against the wall himself, walking home. The overhanging lamps and the general cleanliness were just two of the effects of the initiative.

The courtyard was landscaped; grass, with the occasional shrub or small tree and an ornamental fountain. On one side stood a fenced-off kids' play area. The banked grass sloped down from a central hump to a path that ran round the inner perimeter of the flats with metal steps at each corner of the square leading to the upper floors. Each block of the surrounding flats was identical: concrete, stone-cladded, flat-roofed and six-storeyed. To Nick emerging from the tunnel in the gloaming, following a stint on the back shift, and usually a few drinks in the Swan, the scene always appeared like a surrounding multiplex of screens; the lit-up lounges of each flat showing a different scene from one big soap called Everyday Life.

The bag he carried over his shoulder was a weight. As he walked he slid his thumb under the strap and eased and readjusted the bag. He worked as an electrician at the factory and some tools and equipment he carried to and fro, out of convenience and safekeeping (there had been some thievery in the workshop recently). As he entered the courtyard the shouting swelled and echoed round the buildings. In a corner on the far side a crowd had gathered outside the door of a ground floor flat. It was the sort of bust-up that occurred but with increasing frequency. On the grass slope more people, spread out in small huddles, stood looking on.

Nick sighed again. He could have avoided the crowd had it not been for the timing, or the fact that the congregation was immediately to the left of the metal steps that provided the only access to his flat. He padded across the grass, over the mound and down the slope. The grass was soft underfoot, dark with streaks of light and shadow; looming, stretched, grotesque human shapes. All around the courtyard at the lit-up lounge windows, people were pressed looking out, down at the ongoing row. The shouting continued, voices enjoined in one hysterical piercing grating screaming animal-in-pain racket. Argument and counter-argument. Nick felt the weight of his shoulder bag. He had signed petitions and supported all of the initial measures of the campaign, but, at times, he had began to experience a sort of vague disquiet that he couldn't explain. Even though, as he again reminded himself, this was nothing to do with him.

The crowd outside the flat wasn't as big as the echoing noise had led Nick to expect. There was a main concentrated mob of about thirty but more onlookers on the slope, and then more staring idly from their lounges. Walking down the slope Nick saw a neighbour of his, Ray, who people called Chelsea Ray because he was nuts on the team. Chelsea Ray was standing about forty feet back from the crowd with four other men. He had his arms folded across his chest and his shoulders were hunched and taut. He was wearing the obligatory blue shirt, number 9. Nick didn't like Chelsea Ray. He would sooner have walked on, dipped his head, forced his way through the crowd and dashed for the steps. But as Nick veered right to duck in the shadows, with the aim of approaching the steps from the right of the crowd, Chelsea Ray happened to glance round. Feeling obliged, Nick walked over, drew up alongside him.

Chelsea Ray sideglanced at him. 'Alright. Fucking laugh here, Nick. A right carry on, I'd say. Eh, Don?' The man on Chelsea Ray's left nodded. Nick nodded too and palmed his hair. He sniffed, looked around and down the slope in the direction of the crowd, where everyone else was looking. The shouting kept up. It was almost completely dark now. The crowd were a few feet back from the flat, lit up by the flaring light of the surrounding flats. The light illuminated their faces as if they were near a big bonfire. The door of the surrounded flat was open and he could see several people crammed tight in the hallway. At the head of these, framed in the flat doorway, a woman in a yellow dressing gown stood with her arms folded. Carol. She was shouting, responding to the crowd's taunting and particularly those of a group of women along the front, the crowd leaders. There was a kind of verbal volleying and at each exchange Chelsea Ray and a few of the others chuckled and shook their heads at each other. Nick's feet felt cold. He stamped the ground. Small clouds of breath crossed the cold air. At one point Chelsea Ray shifted, shook his head. He lit up a fag and threw Nick a sideglance.

Nick felt suddenly conscious of having come from work, being slightly grimy and unkempt. Plus, having had the five drinks. He smoothed down his coat, adjusted his bag and cleared his throat.

'So. What started it this time?' he said with affected gravity.

Chelsea Ray looked at Nick. 'Oh it's been coming for a long

time for that slag and her brats! Everyone knows she's been putting it out to tender. And it's got a daughter. Seven years old!' Ray shook his head. 'If I had a daughter seven years old... ' He choked, clenched his fists, sniffed. 'Anyway, that's about the size of it.' He nudged Don – Tottenham Don. 'THAT'S ABOUT THE SIZE OF IT, DON!' he said laughing. Then he turned to Nick again and in a changed serious voice added, 'People can't say they ain't been warned, Nick.' Chelsea Ray, sniffed, shifted, rolled his taut shoulders with a brisk shudder.

Nick waited. He looked down at the crowd, across at the huddled spectators on the grass, up and round at those peering out from their lounge windows. Instead of speaking he made a sort of genial grunt and then walked on. He hurried down the grass slope in the direction of the crowd, towards the steps. As he walked he adjusted his bag, smoothed his hair and felt his chin. He hadn't shaved for three days.

The besieged flat was directly to the left of the steps and the crowd were packed tight in between. Carol had been crying. Nick could see that as he pushed his way through. One morning coming down the steps on the way to work, he had seen her out the front of her flat in the same yellow dressing gown, tying up her bin bags and carrying them across to the collection point. Nick had carried one bag over for her, on his way. Now, as he drew closer he could see her cheeks glistening. And yet her eyes were slits and her lips pursed, defiant. Her mouth was defiant. The way she stood. He wanted to shout to her, above the noise. 'Stand your ground!' The women in the front of the crowd were yelling accusations, raving; shouting, their bodies swaying in repetitive motion, a kind of manic tribal dance. The ringleader – a fat, squat woman Nick recognised from the first TUBY meeting – flushed purple in the glimmering light, stood facing Carol, counting off the charges on the fingers of one hand. A slighter woman alongside her held a clipboard and was brandishing it; edging out from the front of the crowd towards Carol, shaking the petition and then retreating. Carol glared. Nick felt a swell of passion. 'Go on Carol, glare, Carol. Glare!' he wanted to shout. He felt tensed, excited. Carol scanned the crowd narrowing her eyes as if she was a sniper seeking to pick people off, one by one. Nick pushed forward in the thick of bodies, swinging the shoulder bag like a weapon. Behind Carol, crammed in the flat hallway, people stared out with wide rabbit eyes. Nick flinched, ducked, as something thrown from somewhere behind him whizzed past and bounced off the flat wall, near where Carol stood. It was a shoe of all things. 'No!' Carol said. 'Yes!' Someone shouted back with a menacing humour. Then a stone was thrown. Carol's hand shot out and she pointed at the part of the crowd where the stone had come from, in accusation. She stood rigid with her finger pointed. Part of the yellow dressing gown loosened, flapped, exposing the top of one breast. Somebody laughed. Then more laughter. Nick flinched expecting a missile. Someone spat. He heaved, pushed on. He felt breathless. Some people complained at his barging, but they shifted. He pushed through the crowd shouting, 'Let me through, let me through.'

Breaking through he made a dash for the steps. He glanced at Carol as he went. She saw him. He looked straight ahead and ran on.

He felt sick. His stomach churned. There was an alcove at the foot of the metal steps. He paused. The shouting continued behind him, a baying noise. He leaned on the metal step rail, smoothed his hair and adjusted the bag on his shoulder. He shook his head, annoyed. As he did so happened to look away to his left. Carol's flat was to the left of the alcove and a small bedroom window faced out. The curtains were closed but in one corner the curtain had been pulled back slightly. There, staring straight at him out of the darkness, a pair of small black eyes – the daughter. Nick swallowed. He felt suddenly drained. He had had a hard day at work and he felt a headache coming on. Pushing the bag up his shoulder, he ran clattering up the metal steps.

Indoors he threw down the bag. He walked through to the lounge and went straight over to close the curtains. The noise from the courtyard continued but he resisted looking down. Although, as he closed the curtains, he did glance round at the other flats, at the people stood staring. He felt pained, a sour taste in his mouth, a swell of sick. The lounge curtains muffled the noise and blanked the scene. Nick sighed. It had happened before, he thought resignedly, and it would happen again. It was something basic in nature, something deep and instinctive that could not be denied. Although, in his opinion, such situations weren't helped by the authorities who seemed all too willing to exploit and use them to their own advantage. Nick sighed and grinned to himself. He remembered that he had been having this argument with someone at work this very day. And he had had it countless times with his wife, Jan, when she had been around. They would argue at the drop of a hat. Nick felt something else. He glanced at the framed photograph on the wall unit. Jan. Perhaps it was that what drove her away, he thought resignedly, half-amused. He thought back to the argument at work. Even people who were intelligent enough to know better were toeing the government line now, trotting out tired platitudes. Nick sighed again, with exasperation. He felt pained. At times, he despaired.

He flopped down on the sofa. Old despair. At the times when

he despaired he sat with his head in his hands; his hands pressed to his head. Then he'd sigh, sit up, bring out his tin and roll and smoke a little joint. That always improved his mood.

He smoked, keeping it down and letting it go. The noise from the courtyard faded to a faint background buzz. Nick smoked. He held down the smoke and then released it, easily. He looked at the framed photograph of smiling Jan. Josie, their daughter, on her mother's lap. Both smiling. He smiled back. At the photograph. The murmur from the courtyard gradually faded. Maybe it had been a flash in the pan, a mere storm in a teacup that would blow over. Nothing at all. A small, domestic row that had got out of hand. Most likely that was it... Perhaps... Nick closed his eyes. He remembered the staring eyes from the side window, with a small jolt. He closed his eyes. Breathed easily and felt calm, good again. Good. He held in the smoke and then released it, slowly, serenely. Then he had a sudden thought. He leaned across the sofa, picked up the remote, aimed it and clicked on the telly. He buzzed up the volume. It was Park Drive, a soap that the papers were full of but he never watched, or at least not since his wife had left. Now he sat and watched it, bleary-eyed, with the volume up. 'Looks like someone's gone and let the cat out of the bag,' a character said. Nick smiled at that. 'We haven't got a clue whether we're coming or going with these bin bags!' He thought of that. The Park Drive theme blared away, Nick began to doze and then he fell asleep.

He woke up suddenly. Someone had been tap-tapping on the window in his dream and now there was a soft, insistent tapping on his flat door. The telly was on, loud, a chat show. 'And did that amuse you?' 'Well.' He found the remote and killed the sound. He listened. Tap. Tap. Soft taps. He sat upright and looked at the clock. Then he stood up, scooped up the ashtray, carried it through to the kitchen and emptied it in the bin (a small precaution he always took). He hurried down his hallway. At the door he peered out through the spyhole. He looked and looked. The corridor outside was dark and he saw nothing until, looking lower, he saw the eyes, the same eyes, staring back at him from the dark mass. He unchained the door and opened it a touch, smoothing his hair.

'What do you want?' he asked, keeping his voice low.

'We need money,' the girl said.

Nick frowned, puzzled. 'What?'

The girl stared. 'We need money.'

'I haven't got any,' Nick hissed. The girl didn't speak but stared at him and stared. She twisted her hands together. 'I don't have none,' he said, but in a weaker voice. He felt in his pocket. There was some change and a note. He brought out the note and thrust it at her. She grabbed and held it tight. He looked her over; up and down. She was thin and pale. The dress she was wearing, a kind of blue shift dress, was creased and grubby and she had a smudge of grime on her forehead. 'That's all I've got. I'll maybe get some more... Tomorrow... Give you some then,' he said. The little girl stared at him, a hard stare. Then she turned and walked away. He watched her go. As she turned out of sight he looked up and down the dark outer corridor. He listened and then closed his door, quietly.

He passed the ground floor flat the next day, as he came down the steps carrying his heavy bag, on his way to work. He was on the afternoon shift. It was mid morning, a cold but clear day. The courtyard was empty. The flat door was open. He looked around, stopped and then walked over peered in, first down the hallway and then in the lounge window. The flat was empty apart from a few bits of furniture.

'Bit of a ding-dong up your way, I heard.' One of his workmates, the one he had the arguments with, said, as they were knocking off. Nick shrugged. 'Uh huh.' He picked up his heavy bag. The workmate grinned at him, with cheesy triumph. Nick shrugged, walked off to get a drink or two in The Swan, before he caught the bus.

He was smoking his third joint (usually two was his self-imposed limit). There was a knock on the door. Nick clicked off the telly, stood up and went and binned the contents of the ashtray. In the lounge he flapped a newspaper in the air to clear the smoke. He walked down the hall and peered out the spyhole. Two men stood there. Ginger Bob, from the estate, Arsenal Ginger, a friend of Chelsea Ray's. Nick didn't mind Ginger Bob, had always found him friendly. He didn't recognise the bloke with him though. He opened the door.

'Nick.'

'Ginge.' Nick noticed that the other man, who wore a denim jacket over a multi-coloured fancy shirt, was carrying a clipboard. He smoothed his hair, stared at them both, smiling.

'This here is Mike... Mike or Mick Williams – he doesn't mind. Mike's a friend of mine,' Ginger Bob said. 'A friend to us all, really,' he added, turning to Mike Williams.

Mike Williams smiled, glowingly. Nick folded his arms, leaned in this doorway and looked Mike Williams up and down. Despite the weird shirt he was kind of scruffy. He had a large TUBY badge on, plus a card with a photograph of himself with SOCIAL POLICY DEPARTMENT across the top.

Nick smiled. 'Well. Hi Mike or Mick.'

'Hi,' Mike Williams said.

'Look, this is sort of personal, Nick... Any chance that we can come in?' Ginger Bob said, craning to look in the flat.

'No chance!' Nick said quickly grinning. Then he added, 'Nah. Only joking! But you'll have to take me as you find me. I haven't put the hoover round yet!'

'Ha ha,' Ginger Bob said. Mike Williams grinned and nodded.

Nick sat on the armchair. They sat on the sofa.

'How's Chelsea Ray?' Nick said, for something to say.

'He's alright,' Ginger Bob replied.

Mike Williams was looking away, scanning the room. He scanned in the general direction of the wall unit. 'Was that your wife and daughter?' he said.

Nick felt his heart miss a beat. He pushed over his hair. 'Hey, what is this all about?' he said half-smiling. Mike Williams was staring at him a half-smile on his lips. Ginger Bob stared too. Ginger Bob shifted on the sofa. He nodded at the clipboard on Mike William's lap. He cleared his throat.

'Don't take this personal, Nick.' Ginger Bob sighed, paused. 'There's a petition being got up...'

FIVE FAGS AND FOUR CANS OF LAGER

I was wrecked! I'd been having a fight with an old tramp who used to live down our street – the street we lived in when I was a kid. Except that it wasn't our street. Nor was there ever any old tramp. And yet that dream was as real as anything. I remember being in the dream and actually believing in it, there and then, saying to myself in the dream: 'This is no dream, this is here and now.' I remember the old tramp laughing at me, 'Haw haw. Haw haw.' His cracked and stained yellow teeth, bad breath and this overwhelming, decrepit smell. His raucous, persistent laugh. Even as I'd laid into him, punching his arms where he was holding them up in front of his face to defend himself. Trying to get inside his guard. A cackle – that was it – an awful, dry crackling cackle. Haw haw haw. He twisted away. I jumped on him, got him in a half-nelson, forcing his arm up the back of his dirty old donkey jacket. Haw haw. He carried on cackling away. Haw haw haw; demented and decrepitly.

When I woke up all the covers were off the bed and I was sweating heavily. The room smelled, an almost unbearable gaseous putridity. Quiet celebrations are all very well but someone has to go round with a dustpan and brush afterwards.

...There was something else though. Even stranger. Even stranger than fiction. It was quiet.

There was a trapezium of light criss-crossing the ceiling, showing up the microbes of dust and casting a white patch on the stipple effect polytex. This shaft of light squeezed through the tiniest crack in the curtains, like the dusty beam from a projector; narrow and then widening and spreading into the room. It wasn't quiet. There was a noise that, at first, I had taken for quiet. It wasn't though. It was the sound of something else. Something that it took me a while to recognise.

I lay there listening. It was a constant noise. Less of a tick tick tick and more of a gurgle gurgle gurgle. I felt disorientated. Slightly confused. Exhausted. I was soaked with sweat. Listlessness pinning me down.

But just lying there was the easy option. Perhaps that tramp I'd been wrestling with was a symbol of my conscience. (Well? Stranger things have been presented as rational explanation.) I made an effort and spun and sat up on the edge of the bed. Whoops, steady there. Whoo. My shaking feet searched and found my slippers and slid into them. I stood up wobbly, staggered over to the window – starkers, apart from the slippers – pulled at one of the curtains and twisted myself into it, wrapping it round like a toga. A big cloud of pale dust and fluff rose, and, as I freed the curtain, a blinding wave of light flooded in, filling the room like screaming. I closed my eyes stumbled forward, fumbled at the metal catch and, freeing that, edged open the window. (It was one of those full-pane, swivel, suicide-proof window that you could only open so far.) A gust of warm air blew in. Smells. More noise. The window frame creaked on its hinges. I leaned on the sill with my eyes closed tight and then opened them fearlessly and looked. And, what a wondrous sight did my eyes thence behold!

A bouncy castle! In the square! It was yellow, mainly, but with a blue conical turret on top of the tower at each corner. The blue turrets swayed and the whole castle shook warpedly where people were bouncing on the castle's inner floor; bounce, bounce, bounce. Outside, at the entrance to the castle, lay rows of shoes and more people chatting as they anxiously waited their turn.

There was a lot of blue and some stripes of yellow. Elsewhere. And, also elsewhere, down in the square, a multitude of colour and music and things going on. Our flat was on the second floor and the main bedroom and lounge windows faced out to the rear. The wide open square was formed by the backs of the other flats. The flats were in square blocks, three storeys high and brick built with the panel beneath each window painted blue with yellow edging. The window frames were white gloss. Now most of the windows were slanted open and the glass glinted in the light, making an identical reflection along the line of the building, like a string of pearls. Above the grey flat roof of the block opposite the sky was blue. Out of that a bright shimmering yellow sun shone.

In several of the flats directly opposite, in the windows, I could see people moving about, doing various things; reading newspapers, shaking out table cloths and spreading them on tables, hoovering, watching telly. One couple were having a row, jabbing fingers at each other accusingly. Oh well. In the window along from them a man walked across the lounge carrying an LP. He removed the record from its cover, held it up, examined the label and then, holding the disc carefully at the edge, laid it on the deck, lifted over the arm, placed the needle carefully and stepped back. In a while he began to dance; awkward, jerky movements, thrusting out his chin, walking on the spot and whirling his arms in the air. It was the strangest dance I'd ever seen. I laughed at his effort. A sharp stabbing pain jolted across my forehead.

I rubbed my forehead and looked down. In the square two straight concrete paths ran from block to block, crossways, bisecting at the centre. Each quarter of the square, formed by the cross, was flat and grassed over. The bouncy castle was over to the left, wobbling away. People were everywhere. On one square patch of lawn three women in swimsuits lay side by side, sunbathing.

Behind them, on the far side of the square, beneath the open lounge window of one of the first floor flats, on a sort of patio effort, an elderly couple, both wearing white hats – the man in shirt-sleeves and the woman in a knee length flowery dress – sat side by side in deckchairs, drinking tea from cups on saucers. Over to their right, a slim middle aged woman in a white dress was sitting under a yellow parasol, reading a book, her legs curled beneath her and one pale hand flat on the ground. Each time she turned a page she put her nose in the air and sniffed as if to say: 'Yes, I'm the type that reads books. As you can see.'

The paths were clean, as if they had just been swept and the light made shadows so that the grass ranged from dry yellow in the sunlight to a strip of dark green along the back and down the right side where a row of dustbins stood.

Here and there, in pots and window boxes, marigolds, pansies and lobelia bloomed. Kids were playing. Not only on the bouncy castle, or waiting their turn there, but riding bikes, yelling, chasing each other with water-pistols, swinging racquets at shuttlecocks (ball games were not allowed in the square, of course). On one patch of lawn three or four smaller kids laughed and splashed, jumping in and out of an inflatable paddling pool, dripping water on the grass as they raced in circles. Nearby a group of women sat on a step with their arms folded, talking – pausing now and then to shout at the kids before resuming their conversation. The kids carried on regardless: circling, falling down, playing dead, jumping up, falling dead, jumping up. A black cat walked through one of the openings beneath the flats, rubbed against the side of a dustbin, surveyed the scene for a while and changed its mind and retreated huffily. From somewhere a radio was playing, loud dreamy light jazz, an odd but not unpleasant fusion of violin and saxophone. While, floating upwards, came a rich smell of steaming cabbage and onions, accompanied by the sound of mellow lilting laughter.

Two women were sitting side by side on the steps that led down from our block to the square. I knew them. Maureen, from directly below – whom I had always found a bit stand-offish – and Sam, whose door was immediately across from mine. Sam was attractive with short fair hair. She had once brought me a letter that had been delivered to her flat by mistake. 'This letter's addressed to you,' she'd said, standing there in the corridor. 'It was put through my door by mistake. Just one of those things, I suppose. But no postman's perfect.'

Maureen and Sam were chatting, occasionally stopping and glancing across the square to check on their kids, and soaking up the sun. Sam was wearing a light blue halter neck top, white shorts and flip-flops. She had her knees drawn up and her arms hooked round them. An aura of sadness surrounded her. Maureen looked more done-up, with a perm and dressed in a blue jacket and skirt, as if she had been, or was planning on going, out somewhere; to live a little. She sat perched on the edge of the step, so as not to get dust on the skirt.

'Sam,' I hissed. I waved one hand out the narrow gap of the window opening, trying to attract her attention without drawing attention to myself. A few other nosy bastards in the square looked up anyway, and I noticed a bloke staring at me from one of the bedroom windows opposite, leaning nonchalantly, chin in hands, on the sill. Maureen and Sam turned together and looked up. Sam lifted a hand to shield her eyes where the sun reflected off the glass.

'Oh for God's sake! Put something on, Keith.'

I put my finger to my lips, to quieten her. 'Look. Hang on. I'll be down in a minute.'

Maureen shielding her eyes, just stared. 'Well, don't rush on our account!' she said, sniffily. They looked at each other and laughed. Then Maureen looked up again.

'What's with the castle?' I said.

Maureen paused. 'The council laid it on,' she said. 'And there'll be fireworks later... Or, so they say!' With that she turned away. The two women carried on talking.

Fireworks.

I looked across the square. One of the women sunbathing had raised her head and proceeded to gawp. I glared back at her and she pulled a so-so face and lay down again.

In a drawer in the bedroom, the bottom drawer of the wardrobe, I found a pair of shorts. They were the cut down denim shorts that had been fashionable for a while. They were smelling a bit, but more of mustiness than anything nasty. Hurrying, I put the shorts on, tied on a belt and then went into the bathroom. I washed at the sink and dunked my head in the water. I combed my hair and cleaned my teeth. Then I found some deodorant and sprayed under my arms, kept spraying until I smelled of fresh lime and peaches. My beard needed clipping but I forwent that from the time point of view. Back in the bedroom, in the wardrobe, I found a shirt hanging, a clean, ironed, white-cotton shirt just hanging there. I put that on, not bothering to do it up, leaving my chest exposed. (My chest had once been remarked upon as one of my finer points.) Then, still hurrying, I walked through to the lounge and over to the window and glanced out to check that everything was still in place – to convince myself that I hadn't been dreaming. I found my fags on the coffee table, counted them and slid the packet in my shirt pocket. There were five left. I nipped into the kitchen. In the fridge I found four cans of lager – just there, standing on the shelf. I took them and walked down the hall. I walked out of the flat, pulled the door to, double-locked and checked it. Then, whistling as I went, I clattered down the stairs to join the others.

THE FLOOD

They talk about the flood, pulling me into the conversation even though I wasn't there. I couldn't have been. It was the year before I was born. I don't know where I was. As far as I know I didn't exist.

The rain washed down the sides of the valley. The brown flint drift. Light brown mud dislodging the shining flints. Sludge. It rained persistently. A deluge. The valley road became a river again. Fields disappeared underwater. Trees sprouted from lakes.

There is one photograph that I know of. Black and white. Outside the village post office-grocers, a woman is wading, holding high her skirt and coat. She is laughing at the photographer. The shop is just to her right. The water swirls around her thighs.

A lot of the stock from the shop was ruined. The basement flooded and packets of washing powder floated up and out to the river. I imagined it frothing up and when the water subsided, leaving the entire village fresh and sparkling clean.

KEITH MARTIN

Photograph: Rob Weiss

Keith Martin was born in Kent in 1954. After leaving comprehensive school in the late sixties, he worked in a chicken factory,on a
farm, and then as a labourer, hod-carrier, and scaffolder. Always a
keen reader, he took up formal part-time study in the eighties
and obtained an OU Honours degree in Arts, and the Diploma in
Philosophy of the University of Kent.

He recognised an increasing urge to write and began to do so
seriously when laid off as a scaffolder in 1992, at which time he
was a lone parent. Short-listed at the Kent Literary Festival, and a
winner in the Bridport Prize and the Hastings Writers' Group
competitions, he won the 1998 Staple First Editions award for
Short Fiction with the present volume.

Martin's first Staple magazine story was *Nothing Much Happens*
(Spring 1997). His fiction has also appeared in the Bridport Prize
Anthology; and he has published reviews, articles and features in
The Guardian, The New Statesman, and other periodicals.

Keith Martin has been awarded an Arts Council bursary, has
devised and taught philosophy courses for the WEA, is currently a
member of the Labour Party. He lives with his teacher partner,
her children and his daughter, in Gravesend. He plays guitar,
sings, reads and writes every day he is allowed.

A major influence is Chekhov whom Keith Martin first read during a holiday at Pontin's in Dorset in the late eighties:

The kids were off playing on the swings and in the pool, making friends and having a good time. I was in the chalet or sat in the sun reading. After the first story, I thought, 'This isn't a story at all. Where's the ending? What's the point?' Then I read another and another. It was like drinking clear champagne.

Keith Martin would like to acknowledge the comprehensive education system, the Open University and those who have provided encouragement, understanding, love and money.

Staple New Writing

A non-profit-making company, limited by guarantee.

Though no further *collections* can be considered at present, most of the titles in the Staple FIRST EDITION series which are listed overleaf are still in print or have been reprinted. Staple magazine itself continues to welcome poems and short fiction. Founded in 1982, it is published every March, July and December, with a special issue for the annual Staple Open Poetry Competition. Subscription details, Guidelines, and Competition entry forms are available from the address below.

Tor Cottage, 81 Cavendish Road, Matlock, Derbyshire DE4 3HD

Staple First Editions

David Lightfoot	LAST ROUND	1991
Jennifer Olds	THE HALF-ACRE RANCH	1992
Peter Cash	FEN POEMS	1992
Adrienne Brady Ted Burford John Latham Paul Munden David Winwood	QUINTET	1993
Donna Hilbert	WOMEN WHO MAKE MONEY AND THE MEN WHO LOVE THEM	1994
Jennifer Olds	AN EXTRA HALF-ACRE	1995
Julia Casterton Tobias Hill Joan Jobe Smith Huw Watkins Howard Wright Alicia Yerburgh	SESTET	1995
Gregory Warren Wilson	PRESERVING LEMONS	1996
Ruth Sharman Alison Spritzler-Rose Catherine Conzato John Gower	TWO + TWO	1997
Elizabeth Barrett	WALKING ON TIPTOE	1998
Keith Martin	THE ABSOLUTE BOTTOM LINE	1999